GW01066108

Mental

ORLA SHANAGHY

CONTENTS

For Richard, Saorla, Lola,
Ruadhán and Lochlann.

WAVE

Later, in the hospital, the doctors kept asking me how Tim had been that day. Had he given any indication of his state of mind? I rolled back my head, shut my eyes and let the fluorescent ceiling lights burn through my eyelids. Yes, he had been moody. That's Tim.

The squeal of a door hinge made me flinch. I opened my eyes. Another doctor had come into the room – the Psych room in A&E – and was sitting down in the chair on the other side of the table. The table and chairs were bolted to the floor.

"Dr Kenneally," he said without making eye contact. He began turning pages in a cardboard file – Tim's file. He was groomed and clear-skinned. I reached a hand behind me to massage my back.

The doctor leaned back in the chair and finally looked up at me. He crossed one foot over his knee.

"Can you go back to earlier this evening?" he said, clicking out the nib on a pen. "It says here that you and Tim drove from your apartment in town to Tim's parents' house on the coast. You were at the wheel. Why were you the one driving?"

I blinked to soothe the sting in my eyes.

"I always drive," I said.

The doctor started writing.

"Tim doesn't have a licence. He finds driving stressful."

I hadn't eaten or drunk anything for hours. I had to keep swallowing.

The doctor flicked to another page in the file. "You told Dr Browne that it was approximately 7 p.m. this evening when you arrived at the house. What were you planning to do there?"

"Like I told Dr Browne, we have a boat at Tim's parents' house that we're restoring. It used to be his dad's fishing boat. We've been going out there to work on it most evenings after I finish work."

"After you finish work." The doctor paused, pen suspended. "Is Tim in employment?"

"It's difficult for an art teacher. He had a contract but it finished in June."

I had gone through the sequence of events at least three times already. I switched to autopilot. The hospital noises faded and the evening played out before my mind's eye.

The coast road had been gorgeous earlier that evening as we drove into the dusk. The last of the sunlight on our right-hand side threw a splash of gold across the sea. Tim, in the passenger seat, was squinting out the rear window at a house with a boat in the garden. He had seen a man sitting inside the boat.

"Did you see the old guy, Clo? I remember him from when I was a kid. That used to be his fishing boat. He goes out there now to remember the old days." Tim straightened up in his seat and smiled at me. "We'll probably do that, too, when we're old."

That smile. It gets me every time.

Everyone thought the boat was going to be the

making of Tim. His parents gave it to us after several weeks of the summer went by with no sign of a new contract for him. We could see him becoming quieter, going into himself again. In mid-August, his mother made her announcement.

"We're giving you two Daddy's old fishing boat. It's been idle and rotting in that boathouse for years. It'd be a great project for you, Tim. Take your mind off things."

Mary said this with a glance at me. I knew what the glance meant: you need to make this happen.

That was OK by me. Tim and I now owned something substantial together. Okay, not a house, yet – but still, the first big thing that was ours alone.

I didn't need to do much persuading. Tim threw himself into the restoration. When Tim is happy, the world feels wonderful.

At Tim's parents' place, I parked on the gravel at the side of the house and eased myself out of the car. I inhaled through my nose as the sharp breeze licked my face. From behind the house and back garden, I could hear the sea's faint, rhythmic rolling.

"Time to check on our baby," called Tim. He was already halfway across the back garden, a dark figure in the fading light. The back garden is a half-acre stretch of land that leads towards the cliff behind the house and the strand below. The grass is littered with bricks, pieces of wood and other DIY materials belonging to Tim's father. I followed Tim, picking my way.

A metallic bang rang out – Tim pulling back the bolt on the boathouse door. There was a click and a rectangle of light poured onto the grass. The "boathouse" is the McLoughlin term for the weather-beaten outhouse at the back of the site.

Everything was just as we left it yesterday. Mary had meant it when she said the boathouse would be for our use alone. A workbench covered in yellowed Formica stretched the length of the far wall, the rolls of paper with Tim's restoration plans on top of it where we had left them. Fixed shelves were here and there on the bare cement-block walls; tools hung from hooks and brackets. Overhead, saws of various sizes were slotted between the flat felt roof and the supporting wooden beams.

I felt a smile spread across my face as my eyes came to rest on the structure in the middle of the concrete floor. There it was, our baby. Keel up, battered, peeling – but ours. I stroked a hand across the smooth patches on the hull that we had filled yesterday.

Tim was moving around the shed, gathering our equipment. He handed me a wooden block with sandpaper folded around it and picked up a tub of filler and a putty knife for himself. We knelt down side by side on two old cushions and set to work.

Sanding is my job. I worked on yesterday's patches of cured filler, moving my fingertips across each one to check for bumps. Tim searched out more gaps in the boards, pressing putty into them. He placed wax paper over each patch of wet putty, gliding the knife blade across it, then peeling back the paper. I looked at his hands and admired how gracefully they moved, like they do when he paints.

"Beautiful," I said.

Tim met my eye. "I assume you're talking about yourself," he said, putting down his knife and leaning towards me.

I smiled through the kiss. "We said we'd finish the starboard tonight."

He drew me to him. Our hands were already at each other's belt buckles. We pulled off each other's coats. I half-registered the chill of the concrete floor on my thighs. I kicked my jeans off frantically and he pushed into me. I forgot the boat, forgot everything.

I'm not sure how much time passed before we kissed

and rolled apart. Tim got to his feet. I smiled up at him.

"Back to the starboard now, Mr McLaughlin," I said in my exaggerated schoolmistress voice.

He paused in zipping up his jeans and looked down at me, frowning.

"Tim, I was only joking." I pulled on my Converses, jumped to my feet and moved towards him.

Tim looked away. He took the putty knife from where he had left it on the floor and turned to the boat.

"Let's get back to work," he said.

I knew the tone. He had closed down. I hate the way he can make me feel ambushed. Tears pricked my eyes.

I felt the need to escape. Muttering about fresh air, I grabbed my coat off the floor. Tim didn't look up. I slammed the boathouse door behind me.

The wind blew freely this close to the sea. I zipped up my coat, looking left at the light coming from behind the curtains in the house, and right to where the sea hid. The moon was up now and had turned the countryside from gold to a dim silver. I could make out the rough path that led to the cliff edge. I had been down to the shore before, with Tim, in daylight. I started walking.

At the back of the site, the path descended sharply and the sea got louder. I shifted my weight to my right foot and climbed down sideways. Glancing back up towards the boathouse, I saw only the square of yellow light coming from its window. There was no sign of movement. Tim was not coming after me.

I jumped down the last few steps onto the little strand and stepped forward across the stones. Crouching down at the water's edge, I let the water bite my fingers. The waves were breaking forcefully, their loud shushing competing with the wind. I pulled up the hood of my coat. I searched my mind for a word: intimacy. It was just me, the sea and the moonlight.

I smiled into my collar. In college, my friends and I

in business studies used to laugh about the arts students on campus, with their talk of poetry and nature. Then, at a party in someone's flat, I met Tim. He took me to lectures on the Impressionists, to exhibitions at the National Gallery. He read me Keats and Wordsworth and I found myself listening without laughing. I was in love before I realised it.

A wave of that love washed over me. I had been gone a while. It was time to go back.

I pushed open the door of the shed and blinked in the light. Tim was standing with his back to the door, bent over the workbench, head in his hands. He turned. His face was red and contorted.

"Where the fuck were you?"

It took me a moment to take in how he looked and what he had said.

"The . . . the strand. I told you I was going for some air."

"The strand? Remember I told you how dangerous that path is?"

He had told me. I knew that explanations would be useless. I opened my arms and moved towards him. "You were worried. I'm sorry."

Tim stepped towards me, his eyes sunken under the harsh light of the bulb. He was stretching out his right arm. For a second, I thought it was going to be all right. Then I saw that his fingers were gripped around the handle of the putty knife. The tip was pointing at me.

I felt my wider awareness shutting down. The boat, the sandpaper where it lay discarded on the floor, the tools – all were gone. All I could see now were Tim's face, his eyes narrowed and fixed on mine, and the dull metal of the blade.

I opened my mouth.

"Don't say anything," said Tim, "or I'll use it on you."

He lifted his left arm and pulled the blade from wrist to elbow. The soft flesh opened easily. I remember thinking, in a detached way, how beautiful the contrast was between white skin and red blood. He had made a straight line up his forearm. Blood dripped from the gash, forming little splashes of red that glistened on the concrete floor. Tim's knees buckled.

There were screams. I dimly realised they were coming from my mouth. My legs took me out the door and through the darkness, towards the house and light.

Dr Kenneally continued writing for a moment after I stopped talking. He pressed the pen into the paper, made a careful full stop, and looked up at me. His expression had not changed.

"Oh – kay." His falling cadence suggested that a matter had been satisfactorily closed. "You should be able to take Tim home Friday or Saturday, once the wounds have closed up. He'll need the stitches checked about a week after that. His GP can do that, though."

He closed his file and stood up. I blinked.

"Is there something else?" said the doctor.

I swallowed slowly. My head ached.

"Is that it?" I said.

The doctor made a quizzical face.

I tried again. "Tim doesn't have to come back here?"

Dr Kenneally still looked puzzled.

I forced down the lump in my throat.

"Tim could have died tonight," I said slowly. "Are you just going to send him home in a few days? What am I to tell his parents? What if he does the same thing again?"

A distant alarm beeped. There was a rush of footsteps from the corridor and the rattle of a trolley over tiles. Dr Kenneally opened the door. He looked back at me from the doorway.

"If someone is determined to take their own life,

none of us can do anything to prevent that. I'm sorry."

I wanted to rest my arms and head on the table top but couldn't reach. Propping my elbows on my knees, I put my face in my hands and saw Tim three floors above, prostrate under white sheets, eyes closed. A plastic packet on a stand by the bedside dripped blood into a tube, feeding into his right arm.

I will go back to him. I just need some time to figure out what that will mean.

MILK

The first time I saw her, Lisa asked for a twelve-week blow-dry on a bob. I should have known then that something was wrong.

"You know the twelve-week blow-dry is more for longer hair?" I said, bouncing the ends of her bob in my palms, trying to read her face in the mirror. It was a typical Irish October morning – damp you couldn't escape from, the heat from the dryers mixing with the rain the customers walked in.

Lisa, in the chair, was avoiding my eye. "I know. I want it. Let's do it."

I folded my hands together like I was forty and gave the mirror my professional smile.

"You got it, Lisa."

I didn't know Lisa that well. I ended up taking her that time because her usual stylist was out. Then started asking for me. Every few weeks she'd be in, wanting something different. The other stylists thought she was a looper. I did think it was wrong to keep taking her money without saying something. Like, don't mess with your hair so much. But Conor said, "We don't give our clients hairstyles, we give them happiness. Milk it, Amber." And Lisa always looked a bit happier going out of the salon than she did coming in.

So next time she was with me I had her sussed. Bored, loaded yummy mummy, needs excitement. I started giving it loads with my Mallorca nightclub stories.

"You danced on a platform behind a screen?" Her precision-waxed eyebrows nearly disappeared into her hairline.

I was working away at her parting with the colourant and foils, picking out little strands with the handle of the comb. She'd said thin, evenly spaced strands. That takes doing.

"I was a hair stylist in the club. For the house dancers. The dancing was just a side thing. It was hot on the platform all right, but you need the screen. Every so often you get some eejit throwing stuff."

I could see her middle-class face arranging itself, absorbing this. She looked like she never danced in a nightclub in her life. She could have been a knockout – tall, still had a waist, good cheekbones, lovely strong hair – but her dress sense would make you want to cry. Pastel-coloured blouses with cashmere jumpers draped over the shoulders. Her voice was posh, of course – all careful and rounded.

"That must have been hard work," she said. Good breeding, you've got to love it.

"Yeah. Especially after four hours doing the dancers' hair. Once you're up there on the platform you forget being tired, though. You just dance."

Like working in the salon. The bad days are noise, lights, whining clients, aching feet. On the good days, you're strutting around, scissors flying, the clients love you. You're on a stage, giving the clients what they want, feeding their fantasies about themselves. Mam says it's a hard way for a girl to earn a living. Her friend Marie's daughter did the Leaving Cert. Now she sits at a desk all day and gets home for her dinner by six, says Mam when I come in dog tired on late nights.

Lisa was back about three weeks later. I remember it particularly because she was smiling. The whiteness of her teeth nearly took my eye out. She was all, I love this, what do you call it? She was pointing at a model in the magazine she'd brought, with dark roots and golden ends.

My mind was all over the place that day. In my mind I kept seeing skinny girls in silver bikinis, dancing on high platforms, with a sea of eyes staring up at them out of the dark.

"Balayage?"

"Can you do it?"

She wasn't keeping the highlights I'd taken such trouble over. Looper was right. I started getting my equipment ready and searched for something nice to say.

"That's a killer smile you've got there, Lisa," I said. And not even angling for a bigger tip – well, not only. Now that she was actually smiling, I could see that she was one of those people who, when they're happy, it comes out of every pore. I remember noticing that the sun was spilling in the high windows that day, people strolling by in T-shirts, kids ambling along with ice lollies.

"Thanks," said Lisa. She touched her hand to her mouth. "I just got them done. I was worried that they're a bit – you know? Blinding."

I stopped with the colouring brush in mid-air. Lisa's type didn't show insecurity – not to the likes of me, anyway. I cocked my head to one side, letting on to be considering.

"On someone else, maybe," I said. "You've got the skin tone to carry it off."

The smile again. I stopped minding about her not keeping the highlights. I can be a sucker like that. I started chatting away and got to work.

"I guess your mother's just concerned about you," she said after a while, flicking the pages of her magazine. She was looking at photos of celebrity cellulite.

I did a double take in my head. I'd been talking so much I hadn't even realised I'd said that out loud about Mam and her friend Marie's daughter.

Lisa mentioned something about a son before. She didn't talk about him much – I think she said he was away. Boarding school, I assumed. I guessed she must feel guilty about that on some level. Mostly I'm happy to play along when the client wants to work out their issues on you. They pay their money, and in return you're at their disposal. It's no different to dancing in the club.

"Yeah. She's great, my mam," I said. "But the minute I have enough saved for the ticket and a deposit on an apartment, I'm back on the plane to Mallorca. The money is fantastic. Mam needs to chill out." I lower my voice when I say this. Conor thinks I've done my stint abroad and I'm with his salon for good now. I hadn't told anyone I was going back. I wasn't sure why I told Lisa.

I glanced up from painting the colour onto her ends and she was looking at me properly now, magazine in her lap. I was expecting a piece of advice: I should stay where I had a steady job, or go back and do the Leaving Cert to get a better one. I'd heard it all from clients before. Lisa stared for a few seconds. Then she went back to her magazine.

That look of Lisa's stayed with me for the rest of the day. Longer, if I'm honest. I'm not sure why. I'm used to people reacting weirdly when I tell them about dancing in the club in Mallorca. Some are shocked but still want to hear every detail. Others just judge you. I used to not care either way. Now I was bothered by the thought that Lisa might have the wrong idea about me, that she mightn't realise that the dancing was just a means to an end. Like Victor said.

I found myself checking the salon computer to see when she was coming in next. I knew it wouldn't be long.

"I didn't go looking for the dancing job," I said. "It was offered to me."

It was December, the twenty-third, last-minute chaos in the salon. The trainees were dragging their feet around, mopping up melted snow all day. The tinsel and all that other shit had been up for weeks. Lisa wanted Victoria Beckham's new pixie cut for Christmas. I didn't even blink as I sliced through the golden ends it took me two hours to paint on.

"Victor, the head DJ in the club in Mallorca. I met him in January, in Sweat here in town. I couldn't believe it. DJ Victorious, he's been in the charts and everything. In winter he visits clubs all around Europe, scouting for talent."

I was feeling the excitement again just talking about it.

"When he heard I did hair, he asked me right out, did I want to spend the summer in his club in Mallorca, doing the in-house dancers' hair. Told me I could earn in a night what I get in a week here."

Lisa's face, I swear. The most she ever did was raise her eyebrows. "And did you?"

"Yeah, some nights. Once I started dancing. He meant, if you dance as well."

She'd killed my buzz now with her poker face. Where I come from, good manners means responding when someone tells you something, not giving a little nod and saying nothing. That's code, of course, among her lot. It means loser.

By that evening I'd gone from pissed off to raging. We were sitting at the corner table in Sweat: me, Stef, and the rest of the salon staff on our Christmas night out.

"What gives her the right to judge me?" I shouted to Stef over the bass. "You know what she let slip before? She has a fucking degree. And what does she use it for? Sitting around her big house with her kid sent away, looking through magazines for her next hairstyle."

Stef was glancing around the club like always, keeping an eye on who's coming and going. "Relax, will you? She's only a client. You can't take the shit they say seriously."

Normally, I'd agree. But it wasn't what Lisa said so much. It was more an impression she gave. I tried to explain but Stef was pulling me up, towards the dance floor. I was happy to put it out of my mind and feel the crush of bodies close in around me.

On the way home, though, me and Stef dodging piles of slush on the footpaths, I realised that I couldn't put things out of my mind like I used to. I used to get up on a dance floor and think of nothing else. The heat, the thumping of the music, the bodies – it was my element. That's how it was in Mallorca at first. Victor said I was a natural. I remember looking at him across the huge floor as I danced on my platform that first night. The crowd pulsed like one body below. The strobes stroked the tops of their heads, then jumped upwards and sliced the darkness above. Victor met my eye and raised his glass. It was me and him and the crowd, just like he'd said.

Later, when it wasn't as much fun any more and I got scared of people throwing things and guys trying to climb onto the platform, I asked the club manager if I could go back to just doing hair. She said no. They needed dancers. The rent on my room in the apartment was high and I couldn't risk losing the hairdressing gig. I kept dancing.

Now, I can't get rid of the feeling that there's something I can't figure out.

It was when I got home from Sweat that night before Christmas, sipping hot milk to try to get to sleep, that it struck me. It's Lisa. I never thought much about anything that happened in Mallorca before I met her. The questions, the long silences, getting me to go on and on without saying much herself. Was she getting her kicks out of hearing about my life, comparing it to hers, giggling with her friends afterwards about how the other half lives?

I decided then: I didn't care if she was in seven days a week with her mega-tips. I was done with her.

I was back in on the twenty-eighth. The snow was still on the ground. I hated it by this stage. I'd been fizzing away quietly over Christmas, couldn't get the Lisa shit out of my head. I marched right up to Conor at the desk.

"Take Lisa off my list, will you? Stef says she'll do her from now on."

"Lisa, as in, can't-make-her-mind-up Lisa?"

I nodded.

Conor pulled a face. "I phoned her earlier this morning to confirm her next appointment. Her husband answered. Her bloody baby died over Christmas. No more milk from that cash cow." He sighed.

He looked up at me when I didn't move. "You knew her son was in hospital, right?"

The drone of the dryers became muffled. My voice sounded weird in my head. "Her . . . baby? I thought he was away in school."

Conor rolled his eyes. "Duh. He was only ten months or something. In hospital since he was born." He gave me one of his looks. "You can be really self-absorbed sometimes, Amber."

It's March. I got a Facebook message from Victor last night, asking me back this summer. Pay for dancers has gone up, he says. I can stay rent-free in his apartment, he'll make sure I do only the nights I want. Attached to the message is a blurry photo of a girl dancing on a platform in a silver bikini. The picture is dark but I can make out it's me.

I checked the box beside Victor's name and clicked Unfriend.

GRACE

He is the only boy in his class with a sweet shop in his house. The other boys squirm with envy. "Imagine!" they say. "You can sneak down in the night and raid the place!" He used to try to explain. "It's Mammy's shop. I'm not allowed to touch anything." They preferred the fantasy of a sweet-filled playground where he could roam at will.

It is midday in September, dinner time for the people of the town. The hum of the last Angelus bell hangs in the air. Footpaths rattle with the heels of hungry shop girls and office boys. Padraig passes his front door at the end of the row of houses and walks around the corner, arms swinging. The two-minute walk from the school at one end of the street to his house at the other end is a daily happiness, a slice of independence between classroom and home. He is eight, just gone into third class.

He pushes open the shop door at the side of the house and steps in.

The ding of the shop bell is drowned out by men's voices coming from the dining room behind the shop. He lingers by the shelf with the satin cushions, plump and gleaming in their glass jars.

"Padraig, is that you?" Mammy puts her head around the door behind the cash register. Her hair stands up around her forehead and her face is flushed. She is holding a steaming plate of food. "Come and have your dinner. Maggie needs to finish the dishes."

He walks through the dining room without stopping and into the kitchen at the back of the house. It is steaming hot and smells of boiled cabbage, but it is away from the lodgers, country men who live and work in the town, back on their dinner hour. They laugh too loudly and ask questions he doesn't understand. In the kitchen, he has peace.

Mammy spins between kitchen and dining room, serving the lodgers, plates held high. Maggie works silently at the sink, washing the crockery that Mammy brings. He watches Mammy's face each time she comes in. She casts glances at him, checking that he is eating, but her eyes flick away.

"Is Daddy coming home for his dinner?" he asks. She doesn't seem to hear. There is a call for mustard from the dining room and she is gone again.

Maggie turns her head to him over her shoulder, her reddened arms half-hidden in suds. "He's not at the building site today, he's in working next door. Don't be at him now. He's like ninety divils."

He slides his empty plate and cutlery into the sink and retreats upstairs, walking along the upstairs passage and through the doorway into the house next door.

This is another fascination for the boys in school. His parents bought the house next door three years ago, after the elderly widow in it died. He remembered asking why they needed another house that was stuck onto their own. He received no clear answer. His father knocked holes in the walls and made two doorways between the houses, one just inside the front door, the other connecting the two upstairs passages.

At first, he ran joyful circuits, up one stairs, along the extended passage, and down the other stairs next door. Then more lodgers started to arrive in the new house; the old spare room already held two. The ones next door had their own sitting-room and their own kitchen if they wanted tea at night. He heard his mother tell his father that their lodgers were the envy of the town. The more men came, the louder they got. He stopped the circuits.

He stands, hands in pockets, at the window in the upstairs passage. The lodgers don't come up here at dinner time. He looks down on the two back yards, still separated by a brick wall. He hopes his father never knocks down that wall; the lodgers have their own garden, and he and his parents have theirs. On summer and autumn evenings, his mother brings out the long, hard-backed copybooks where she writes everything about the shop and sits and tots up figures while he lies on his stomach in the grass, reading.

His father comes in late from the building site, the day's dust in his hair. He sinks into one of the rickety deck-chairs and lets his hard hat thud onto the grass.

"When you grow up, get a job in the civil service, Padraig boy. Running your own business is a mug's game."

His mother gets up wordlessly, comes back with a bottle of white lemonade from the shelf in the shop, and places it in his father's hand.

He is brought back to the present by his parents' muffled voices floating up from downstairs, with the rising inflections of an argument. After a few minutes there is silence and he relaxes. Then a banging, crunching sound splits the air.

He runs to the top of the next-door stairs. Looking down, he sees the shiny top of his father's head. His father is standing by the bottom step with the sledgehammer resting on its head on the floor beside him. His head is bowed, his eyes closed, one hand on his hip, the other resting on the end of the sledgehammer. The lower part of the banisters is gone. There is a pile of splintered wood at his feet.

Padraig prepares his question, monitoring his father.

"Why are you breaking the stairs, Daddy?"

His father does not look up. He pulls an arm slowly across his brow.

"To make room in here for Mammy's café."

The front door slams. The lodgers are gone back to work. The only sound now is his father breathing heavily through his nose. There is a movement behind his father and Padraig inches down a few steps to see. It is his mother. She stands in the downstairs doorway between the two houses, tea towel in one hand, looking around silently. His father does not move. Padraig looks down on them standing there, the rubble of wood and dust at their feet. He longs for them to say something, but they just stand and look.

When he comes home from school later that afternoon, the house is quiet. He sits at the desk by the window in his bedroom, writing in his school copy books, when voices again leak through the walls. It is an angry duet, one voice low and tense, the other high and insistent. Padraig's stomach tightens.

The crescendo of argument builds. A door is wrenched open. He knows the sound of every door in the house: it is his parents' bedroom. He opens his own bedroom door and looks out into the passage. He catches sight of his father, disappearing down the stairs, holding an armful of papers. The front door opens, then he hears the key in the door of their car. A few seconds later his father is going back into his bedroom again, emerging with more papers. He doesn't seem to register Padraig's presence as he passes back and forth. An unfamiliar sound hits Padraig's ears a few seconds before he realises it is his father, shouting from the hall downstairs.

"You've taken over this whole house with your shop and your lodgers and now your bloody café. By God, you'll not take over the business my father built up as well."

His mother bursts through the bedroom door, hair wild. She clatters down the stairs in her heels after his father. Padraig's throat contracts with fear that she will fall.

"Have you looked in those ledgers? It'll not be a business much longer at that rate. Is it any wonder that I have to keep thinking of ways to bring money into this house?"

Padraig peers around the top of the stairs. He sees the tops of both their heads, his father standing on the front step clutching the papers to his chest, looking back through the open front door at his wife in the hall, her left hand resting on the stair post. The afternoon sun is coming in the front door and falls as a lake of yellow light on the stone floor at her feet.

"All this paperwork for the building company is going to the site office." His father's face is grim. "You'll not get your hands on these again." He disappears out to the car.

Padraig's mother turns and carefully treads each step back up the stairs. He moves back to let her pass. Her bedroom door closes softly behind her. For a reason he cannot name, that softness upsets him most of all.

He stays in his room then, bent over his books. The voices go on, quieter now, and doors keep opening and shutting, but he no longer wants to decipher their meaning.

He looks up at the sound of the handle turning on his

bedroom door. His mother's face in the doorway is like a doll's, eyes wide and bright. She is wearing her good blue wool coat.

"Come on, Padraig. We're going for a drive."

"But it's nearly six o'clock. Won't the lodgers be wanting their tea?"

"Maggie'll look after them. Hurry, Daddy's got the car started."

Most of his friends' parents do not own a car. He usually dislikes driving through the town with the roar of the engine attracting attention. Today he is glad that it fills the silence in the car. His father palms the gear stick slowly and deliberately, staring straight ahead. His mother jabs on the radio, then sits looking mutely out her window. Padraig slides from side to side on the leather back seat, looking first out one window, then the other, glancing all the time at the backs of his parents' heads, watching.

They are in the countryside in minutes, the road narrowing between stone walls. Theirs is the only car on the road. The sun has passed its peak and casts gold-green light over the fields. A word from a poem learned at school surfaces in his mind: radiant. He casts the word around in his mind.

His mother turns up the dial on the radio. At first, it is as if she is singing only to herself as she gazes out across the countryside. Then she turns in her seat to face his father, her voice becoming louder. She leans forward to make sure she is in his father's sight and cocks her head comically to one side as she sings, rolling her eyes flirtatiously. His father's shoulders shake slightly. Padraig sees a crinkle at the side of his face. He turns his head to Padraig's mother, trying to frown as if to suppress the laughter that finally bursts from him and shakes his whole upper body. "You'll not get me to sing that drivel, Grace girl."

Padraig's mother is leaning across the gear stick. She takes hold of her husband's arm and puts her head on his shoulder. "Sing with me, Tom boy."

"And that is why the poets always write
If there's a new moon bright above
It's cherry pink and apple blossom white
When you're in love."

Padraig sits still now, watching from the seat behind as his father reaches an arm across his mother's shoulders and pulls her close, their heads together as the gold-lit road unfolds in front of them.

SAW

Funny how, after all these years, they still ended up sitting in the kitchen. Fergal ran his palm across the old Formica table top. They had lived their lives at this table, he and his brothers and sisters. His mother had often declared it was a piece of rubbish and that she was getting a new one, but she never did.

"Now." His mother placed a mug of pale tea in front of him. "No sugar, like you asked." She hovered behind him, radiating disapproval, he felt sure, of his new preference.

"Will you not sit down, Mammy," he said to his mug.

She did so as he knew she would, sliding sideways onto the seat and perching on one edge, as if she expected to rise again at any moment.

She said, "Your father tells me . . ." at the same time as he began, "Did Daddy tell you . . ."

An uncertain smile passed and faded between them.

"Congratulations," said Fergal's mother. "A child is a gift." She took a sip from her mug. "Even the fifth one."

He had known that a dart would come. He kept his breathing slow, like he had practised.

"Due in February," he said. "We're delighted." He swallowed a mouthful of tea.

"So was this one a happy accident too?" His mother had wound her legs around each other, knees and ankles, with her free arm clutched across her rib cage.

Breathe, Fergal. Breathe.

"None of the children Fiona and I have were accidents, Mammy. They're wanted, every one."

Fergal pushed back his chair and crossed the kitchen to look out the window. His parents' back yard had been a work in progress as long as he could remember. Peering through the twilight, he could make out the irregular beginnings of a cement block wall jutting up from a square of poured concrete on the ground to his right, opposite his father's workshop.

"Daddy's been busy," he said without turning around.

He heard his mother shift in her chair. He swallowed away a lump in his throat. Had they nothing to say to each other? His own mother, who had carried him for nine months. He was the first; four more came after. She always gave the impression that child-rearing was a cross to be borne.

A child was a gift. But gifts could be unwanted.

Fergal gripped the edge of the sink.

"You can't unwant your own grandchild."

Silence came from behind him.

"What?"

He turned around and looked at his mother straight on for the first time since he'd come in the door. All the years he had been away in London, she had loomed large in his mind. She had been a force sweeping through their house, one that he and his siblings both feared and loved. Now, sitting at the kitchen table, she looked small. A bird of a woman, he remembered a neighbour saying about her years ago.

"I said you can't unwant your own grandchild. Feel

whatever you want about your own children. But mine, no way."

"You pup." His mother's mouth had tightened into a point, lines radiating from it like spokes in a wheel. "You little pup."

He nodded slowly, his hands feeling for the edge of the sink behind him.

"Maybe you would've liked that. Pups that could be put in a sack and drowned."

Fergal's heart was off, racing, and with it came the swimming in his head. He moved forward for his chair, but staggered. His head caught the corner of the table as he went down.

"Jesus." The word came from somewhere above him. Chair legs scraped against lino.

A hand swept his forehead and lifted his eyelids one after the other.

"I'm all right." Fergal rolled onto his side and with his mother's help, got back into his chair. After gripping both his arms for a moment, as if she could prevent him from falling again, his mother moved to the fridge. She pressed ice cubes into a tea towel, parcelled it up, and handed it to him. He held it to the pain that blossomed from his forehead.

"You still get the fainting fits," said Fergal's mother, sliding back into her chair and taking an abrupt swallow of tea.

Fergal shook his head, then winced. "They're not fainting fits, Mammy. They're . . . they're panic attacks."

He let the statement hang in the air. He knew his mother's views on mental illness. "Some of us don't have the luxury of a nervous breakdown," he had heard her say to his father years ago about a cousin who was in St Patrick's Hospital.

Fergal saw with sudden insight that he might never talk to his mother like this again.

"I have clinical depression, Mammy. The panic attacks go with it. I saw a psychotherapist for years in London. I take medication. That, and Fiona and the children, saved me."

His mother had not moved except for one hand that was now at her forehead. As Fergal looked at her, light from the fluorescent strip in the ceiling glinted off the silver of her hair.

Fergal felt a profound tiredness wash over every part of his body.

"I'll be off, so," he said, standing carefully and carrying the bunched-up tea towel to the sink. The ice cubes clattered against the metal. Through the window, he saw the brick work of the half-finished shed silhouetted in right angles against the flare of the dying sun.

The crunching of heavy rubber on gravel cut through the silence. Fergal found himself staying by the sink, listening. The sound was lodged in his memory from earliest childhood: his father arriving home in the articulated truck when he and the other children were in bed. Fergal noticed the sound wherever he was: the teenage summer picking fruit in Bavaria, the year waiting tables in Cape May, the countless nights in bed beside Fiona in their tiny flat in Tooting. Every time he heard the hiss of a truck's parking brake, he felt a sense of homecoming.

He felt his heart lift despite himself, and turned towards the kitchen door in greeting. But the door handle did not move. Turning back to the window, he saw his father's dim, slightly stooped figure heading in the opposite direction, towards the workshop at the left-hand side of the back yard.

There was the familiar squeak of hinges, then the light went on in the workshop window. A few seconds later, Fergal heard the whine of the bench saw.

He turned towards his mother.

"What in the name of God is Daddy at?" he said.

His mother was still in the same position, eyes fixed on the table top. She sighed.

"Sure you know what he's at. Same as always – his latest project. That new shed." She gestured in the direction of the garden.

Fergal stared. "You mean he still does that? At his age, after a day in the truck?"

His mother raised her eyes and looked at him levelly. He shifted. It struck him that his discomfort could be because he, like all his siblings, was unused to their mother looking for long at any of them.

"Your father's sixty-two," said his mother. "He's in better health than any of us."

Fergal looked away from his mother. He wanted to leave. But the urge for knowledge was in him, ferreting in his memory for fragments. Staring down at the faded lino, feeling the throbbing in his forehead, he saw his father there, years ago, prostrate. The big stove-top kettle lay where it had fallen from his father's hand, the lino shrivelling under the heat and giving off an acrid smell. Fergal – he must have been eight or nine – looked down at his father's gasping, clutching body and the pool of hot water spreading out on the floor beside him.

Another image pushed its way through. His father, again on the floor, this time in the workshop. Fergal must have been in his mid-teens. His head was full of noise: the bench saw whined shrilly, running empty. A large timber board, cut part-way through, lay on the floor. There was another noise above that of the saw, the noise that had alerted him to come running. His father lay sprawled against the wall, clutching one hand to his chest, his mouth wrenched open. His hands and arms glistened dark red. The noise was Fergal's father, screaming.

Fergal's eyelids begged to close but he forced his head up to look back at his mother.

"Daddy gets the attacks too, doesn't he? Does he have depression?"

His mother tightened her arms around her rib cage. She nodded once, slowly.

Fergal drank in air and let it out again. Darkness had fallen fully by now. He looked at himself and his mother reflected in the blackness of the window.

He summoned a last piece of strength.

"When you feel you can be happy about the baby, Mammy, come over and see us."

Fergal closed the back door quietly. The night air was cool in his lungs. He walked across the gravel to his car, clutching his new knowledge inside him.

ASK JESSICA

I like the curtains in my bedroom. The fabric is heavy and shuts out the light. Their colour is organic vellum. I picked it from the catalogue.

I'm standing by the window, holding aside a curtain, peering out onto the driveway below. A car is parked outside our gate. A woman is climbing out of the passenger side. The car's paint work has lost its gloss; it swallows up the sunlight. The car moves off and Magda walks up our driveway, out of sight.

I let the curtain fall back and stand in the darkened room, waiting for the doorbell.

I wasn't always like this. My parents used to say I was a "goer". I was the social organiser of my class in college. If someone needed to know where we were going that night, people would say "Ask Jessica."

I pull open the front door.

"Magda, nice to see you!"

You should see me with my game face on.

"How are you today? Still tired?" says Magda, smiling, as she steps inside.

She makes such firm eye contact. I pick something off my sleeve.

"I'm fine," I say. I move towards the kitchen and begin listing what I need her to do that day: iron Mark's shirts, hoover, dust, sort the laundry.

Magda follows me into the kitchen and crouches down at the cupboard under the sink, taking out the cleaning things. I glance at her and feel pity. She is forty-four, only three years older than me. Her face is lined and pale. Her hair glows a brassy maroon under the skylight. All over her scalp I see a crop of white roots.

Magda stands up with the container of cleaning things in her hands. I'm beginning to get edgy now, being downstairs.

"That's about it," I say, looking around. I head for the door. "Oh. My friend Heather is coming by around eleven to pick up the cake for the school bake sale." I gesture to the cake box on the kitchen counter. "Can you give it to her, please? I'll be resting."

I make my escape up the stairs, past the framed photographs ascending the wall. The bedroom door clicks closed behind me. I get into bed and look at the clock radio on Mark's night stand. It's ten past ten. In just under five hours, Emma and Lorcan will arrive home from school on the bus. I sink back into the pillows and close my eyes.

Clinical depression. I got my diagnosis a month ago. Sitting beside Mark that day in the psychiatrist's office, it was like we had heard two different things. Mark sat back into his chair and nodded. I recoiled inside. Mark and the doctor started talking about medication. Their voices came to me as if under water.

In the car on the way home, Mark was practically chirpy.

"This is what we hoped for, love. A definite diagnosis. Something we can start solving. Right?"

I twisted my hands and said nothing.

It was our ritual when we arrived home from somewhere to sit in the kitchen, drinking tea and chatting. That day, I went in the front door and straight up the stairs to bed. I knew I was hurting Mark. I couldn't help it. I craved darkness and silence.

I'm officially mad, I thought. Who will trust me now?

The muffled hum of the hoover starts downstairs. I picture Magda moving through the rooms, pushing the hoover head along the carpet in front of her. The living room, the dining room, the playroom, the study. She would switch to the hard-floor head for the kitchen, the utility room and the hall. Morning sunlight would be streaming in the windows at the front of the house. I shudder, thinking of all that bright, open space. An image pushes itself into my mind, of the road outside our house, the fields behind it, the lane that runs between the fields and beyond all that, a glistening hint of the sea.

A crawling feeling is advancing like a slow tide over my scalp and neck. I pull open the bedside drawer and feel around for my pills. I push two out of the foil and swallow them.

I haven't been out of bed much in a while. A long while. Since the day of the diagnosis. I lie here and roll the words around in my head: clinical depression. They summon up images of hunched, ashen-faced people sitting alone by windows. I was school head girl. I was president of the college debating society. I was a working mother and chairperson of the Parents' Association. Long-term illness doesn't fit into that picture. Mental illness even less so.

The boxes of pills lay in the drawer for a while. At first, I told myself it was by no means certain that I had what the doctor had said. Another specialist might be more of my opinion: I was simply worn out from the demands of work and parenthood, that all I needed was some rest. I had been neglecting myself; a spa break would surely help.

Mark found the unopened boxes.

"You have an illness. This is the medicine for that illness," he said.

Hearing the quiver in his voice, I got a glimpse of how serious this might be. I started taking the medicine.

It eased the heart palpitations, the breathlessness, the trembling. Mark was happy to see an improvement. The fear stayed with me. Fear that anyone would find out, that my friends would drop me, that people would treat me like a mental patient. I stayed inside. I communicated by text and Facebook. As long as nobody saw me, I felt safe.

But the children. We live in the same house. They know something is going on. They used to burst in the door from school. Emma would fling her bag in a corner and start singing along with her iPod. Lorcan would head straight for the fridge, complaining loudly about this teacher or that school friend. Now they step in quietly. Mark gave Lorcan a key. They busy themselves in the kitchen, then tiptoe upstairs with a cup of tea and a biscuit for me.

Their eyes, their faces. I can't think about it now.

I hear sounds from the stairwell. Magda is dusting the picture frames. Mark insists on keeping those pictures up. Graduation day. Wedding day. Honeymoon. Bringing Lorcan home for the first time, then Emma. My own face smiles down at me from frame after frame, mocking me. Look how you used to be.

I'm the only one who sees the strain in my smiles in the pictures. As Lorcan clung to my chest moments after his birth, coated in white vernix, his tiny mouth already open, I was stunned. How could such love be accompanied by such anger? The pain of labour left me enraged. I wanted to tell anyone and everyone about the pain I had just endured. People patted my hand and said the main thing was that the baby was healthy.

It was one of the main things. It wasn't the only thing. I knew I had just done something remarkable. I felt like an endurance athlete or a survivor of some cataclysmic natural disaster. Nobody else seemed to see it that way. The tear that Lorcan's head left in me healed in days. Nobody wanted to hear about the wound in my mind.

Mark was so kind about what I had been through, but it hadn't been him in agony; he didn't understand how deep it went. After a few days, I stopped mentioning it.

The second time round, I swore in disbelief as the contractions forced me to my hands and knees on the bedroom floor. It really was this bad; I hadn't been misremembering. Creating new life would be the death of me.

A knock at the door startles me and I jerk upright in bed. Magda comes in holding the spray can of furniture polish.

"Polish empty," she says from the doorway. "You get more for next time?"

I stammer a reply. The pills relax me so much.

Magda is still standing by the door, squinting at me in the half-light.

"Maybe you see doctor?" she says. "Many weeks you so tired, always in bed."

I mumble something vague and she goes. I collapse gratefully back onto the pillows. I know she's kind but I don't want kindness. I want to be left alone.

A wonderful effect of the pills is that I'm starting to remember things again. I close my eyes and drift back to where I had been before Magda came in. The beach in Worthing, Barbados, where Mark and I went on honeymoon. I'm standing on warm, champagne-coloured sand, my arms raised to the sun. The breeze is gentle on my face. Mark is sitting farther back, in the shade of a tree, laughing. He opens his arms and I run into them.

I become aware of someone shaking my arm. My eyes focus slowly. Magda's face floats over me.

"Jessica," she's saying. "I have call from school. My son sick. I need go now, collect him. See you next week, yes?"

Her eyes move to the bedside table. The little tray of pills lies there, bits of jagged foil sticking up. She looks back at me. She gives me a hug, bending low over the bed. I try to reciprocate.

The front door bangs shut after her. My head swims now from being abruptly woken, twice. I catch sight of myself in the mirror on my vanity at the other side of the room. The woman who stares back is a pale figure in an old T-shirt, with lank, matted hair. I look away. My eyes glance over the clock radio. Ten fifty-five.

Heather. The cake. Magda is gone. I will have to open the door myself.

The kitchen seems more pristine and gleaming than ever after the gloom of the bedroom. I lift the lid of the cardboard box on the worktop. The cake sits inside, white-iced and perfect. I pull the cardboard tabs out of their slots and stare at the cake for a minute.

The back garden is pristine, too. I stop at the back door, taken aback. I haven't been outside in a while. It's so quiet; it's a weekday morning and the suburbs are empty. The only sounds are unseen birds and the engine of a passing car.

I lift the lid of the organic waste bin and dump in the cake. The bin is almost full with grass cuttings and the cake lands upside-down but whole. Then the cuttings start to shift under its weight. The cake sags and separates into pieces. I stand there for a moment.

Sadness fills me for the destruction of something so perfect.

I hurry back inside. The bedroom is so soothing and unstimulating; the outside world is making my senses reel. Panic rises in my throat. I cast about me in the utility room. What do you need to leave the house?

My eye falls on the row of wellington boots on the floor beside the washing machine. I pull on the biggest pair, then grab the biggest coat from a hook on the door. It is Mark's old wax jacket, the one he used to wear for hiking. A row of beautiful ladies' coats hangs in the wardrobe upstairs in their plastic dry-cleaning sheaths, but I'm not going back up there. I have to move forward.

I close the front door slowly behind me. I stand on the front step and looked vaguely around me. Shit. I've forgotten my car keys. My eyes rake across the empty driveway. Where is my car? After a moment, a memory surfaces. I am sitting up in bed, with Mark sitting on the edge of the bed, my hands in his. Oh yes. I have missed so much work in the past few months that he has had to tell my boss I'm not coming back. We are a one-income family now. He has to sell my car.

A passing car honks as I step gingerly along the footpath. I see young men's faces in the windows, heads thrown back. Laughter comes to me across the air. I look down and realise that the wax jacket is hanging open, and underneath I am wearing only a T-shirt and wellies.

The route is coming back to me as I walk. I cross the road at the traffic lights. I turn left, then right. The sun is shining but I feel incredibly cold; I shove my fists into my coat pockets. I turn into the grassy lane that leads down to the harbour. I'm glad to be off the roads now, away from the house where Heather will call any minute.

The lane is nice and empty. I walk faster, nonetheless. I remember how, when we moved to this area as newlyweds, Mark and I were so happy to live close to the sea.

I turn a bend in the lane. There it is, the sea, glittering in the sunshine, wrinkling in the breeze. The pier stretches out like a welcoming arm, sheltering fishing boats and dinghies. I stop to catch my breath and shield my eyes with my hand. The end of the pier looks very far away.

The muscles in my neck stiffen. Someone is running. Behind me. Towards me.

"Jessica!" A hand on my shoulder, then another on my other shoulder, turning me gently around. A pair of gym shoes, legs in Lycra yoga pants. A kind, frowning face. Heather.

"You walked in front of me at the lights on my way over. I pulled in at Spar." Heather's eyes make contact with mine. "Are you OK?"

The sun is blazing now. It pierces the edge of my field of vision. Everything becomes fluid, blurred. Arms move around me. Heather's jacket rustles against mine. I bury my face in the fabric on her shoulder.

ACKNOWLEDGMENTS

Heartfelt thanks to:

Richard Rodger, for his unfailing faith in me, especially when my own was flagging.

Saorla, Lola, Ruadhán and **Lochlann**, for keeping me real and not caring about 'Mom's book'.

Kay and **Noel Shanaghy**, for their support and encouragement in many forms, over many years.

Conor, Eóin and **Niall Shanaghy**, first victims of my early attempts at playwriting, and unstinting supporters for more years than we care to remember.

Noreen and **Hamish Rodger**, for huge amounts of help, support and encouragement.

Lauren and **Jack Dunstan**, for inspiration and helping me keep the dream alive.

Dawn Shanaghy, Keelin Murphy and **Sharon Shanaghy** for years of sisterly support and encouragement.

Monica Carroll, Annette Sheehan, Ger Healion, Mary Carpenter, DJ Shanaghy, Kay Shanaghy ('Auntie Kay') and their families, for all their support.

Susanna Fitzgerald, Niam Savage, Nina Walsh and **Marie Keating**, for many years of friendship, support and encouragement.

Monica Jackman, Brendan Jackman, Vivienne Griffin, Leela O'Shea, Claire Bulfin, Lisa Mullally, Siobhán Smyth RIP, Shauna Lineen, Marika Dunne, Lynn Mulvihill, Derek Flynn, Joan Power, Jim O'Donnell and **Helga O'Donnell** for support and for turning up at my events.

My beta readers **Harriet Baldwin, Richard Brewis, Vivienne Griffin, Keelin Murphy, Jessica Noone, Leela O'Shea, Conor Shanaghy, Eóin Shanaghy** and **Megan Stewart**.

My editors **Robert Doran** and **Alison Walsh** for their

painstaking work and valuable feedback.

Derbhile Graham, supporter, advisor, cheerleader, friend, writer.

Denis O'Shea, my primary school English teacher and former school principal at Faithlegg National School, for nurturing my writing and encouraging me to believe in myself.

Don Divine, my English teacher at St. Angela's secondary school, Waterford, for encouraging my writing and supporting my love of English.

Eleanor Tubbritt, my Transition Year English teacher at St. Angela's secondary school, Waterford, for her encouragement and support in producing my first 'novella'.

Edward Deniston, poet and educator, for inspiring me on a visit to my secondary school and subsequently providing valuable encouragement and advice in my teen years.

Fintan Power and **PJ McAuliffe**, writers and leading figures in the Waterford writing community, for helping me to return to writing as an adult, and for giving me a platform.

Karen Sarah Moore, Lynn Mulvihill and **Liz Walsh** of Write Club, for valuable support, feedback and encouragement.

Admins and members of the Facebook group **Irish Writers, Editors and Publishing Professionals**, for their highly useful posts and responses.

Mark Roper, poet and educator, for his ongoing encouragement and support over many years.

Clíona ní Anluain of RTÉ Radio, for giving me the opportunity to read my work on national radio and including a piece of mine in *Sunday Miscellany Anthology 2008 - 2011*.

Ruth Buchanan, formerly of RTÉ Radio and host of 1980s radio show 'Poparama', for broadcasting my first piece on national radio when I was eight years old.

Gay Byrne, iconic broadcaster on RTÉ radio and television, for reading a piece of mine on Lyric FM.

Maria McCann of WLR FM, for giving me a chance on air, for naming my blog(!) and for believing in me and my work.

Roald Dahl RIP, for replying to my letter and showing me that dreams do come true.

Sinéad Gleeson, writer, editor, journalist and presenter of RTÉ Radio One's *The Book Show*, for generosity and encouragement.

Nuala ní Chonchúir a.k.a. Nuala O'Connor, writer and writing tutor, for hugely valuable advice and guidance.

Vanessa O'Loughlin of writing.ie for support, advice and positivity, and for encouraging me to speak at literary festivals.

And lastly:

Santa Claus, for leaving a typewriter under the Christmas tree.

ABOUT THE AUTHOR

Orla Shanaghy was born in Waterford, Ireland, where she lives. This is her first book.

Find out more at www.waittilitellyou.com and on social media under Orla Shanaghy.

67583609R00033

Made in the USA
Charleston, SC
18 February 2017